ASL Tales

The Boy Who Cried Wolf!

Retold by Susan Schaller • Illustrated by Connie Clanton
Performed by H. Dee Clanton

ASLTales

Dublin, NH

The Publisher, Author, Illustrator and ASL Artist would like to thank
Tony Bonjorno, Karen Braz, Alisha Bronk, Marianne Dethier,
Yvonne Lauzière, Alicia Papanek, Susan Reiners, Real Gilbert of
WORDS Foreign Language Translation and Interpreting Services,
Joe Biedrzycki of Studio B, all of the translators
and the rest of the ASL Tales Team.

First Edition 2013

ISBN 978-0-9818139-1-2

Design by Yvonne Lauzière
ASL Consultation by Pinky Aiello and Alisha Bronk
Videography by Yoon Lee

Visit us at ASLTales.net

To our daughter Natalie:

*As a child your fascination and imitation
of ASL stories, like the Twelve Dancing Princesses,
proved the importance of ASL in a child's development in
all aspects of life from linguistics to simply imagination.*

~ Connie and Dee Clanton ~

*In memory of Lou Fant who, along with Deaf people,
introduced me to my face, and taught me how to see better.*

~ Susan Schaller ~

A long time ago
a boy sat on a hill
and watched
sheep all day.

1

He sat
on a
big rock
and
watched.

He sat on
the grass
and
watched.

He rolled onto his
tummy and watched.

The boy was bored.

He lay on his tummy
and counted sheep.

He lay on his side
and watched sheep.

"I'll roll
down
the hill."

He rolled and tumbled and
tumbled and rolled and
got covered with grass.

4

But he was still bored.

"I'll dance."

He danced and danced.

He climbed a tree to a big branch
and plopped down onto it.

He sat swinging
his legs.

He looked
around.

He jumped out
of the tree.

He stood on his
hands until he
fell down and
got covered with
grass again.

And... he was still bored.

7

He stood on a big rock
and waved his arms.

"Wolf! Help!
The wolf is here!"

he cried.

The villagers looked up.
They came running as fast as they could.

"Where,
where?"
they asked.

"Where is the wolf?"

"There's no wolf here.
I was just having fun!"

"What? No wolf?"

A skinny old
woman shook
her fist.

A farmer
stomped
his foot.

A little girl
stuck out
her tongue.

The boy's
big brother
frowned.

No one was happy.

After that, the boy did try to be good.

He tried
rolling down
the hill.

He tried
whistling.

He tried
dancing.

But he was still bored.

He went back up the hill.

"Wolf! Help! The wolf is here!"

Again, the villagers looked up.
Again, the villagers came running.
Again they asked,

"Where?
Where is the wolf?"

And again,
the boy laughed
at them.

There was still no wolf.

The skinny old
woman shook
both her fists.

The farmer
threw down
his hat.

The little girl
hopped up
and down.

The boy's
big brother
chased him.

Then the villagers
shouted at the boy,

"Don't cry wolf if there is no wolf!"

And they all went down the hill.

"I was just playing,"
the boy whined.

He sat on the rock,
feeling sorry for himself.

He looked around and saw
something moving - something
with long ears and squinty eyes
and sharp teeth!

It was...a...WOLF!!!

"WOLF, WOLF!! HELP!!!"
he cried.

The skinny old woman did not go.
The farmer did not go.
The little girl did not go.
The boy's big brother did not go.

No one came.
All the sheep were gone.

26

The boy was not bored now.
He was sad.

He never lied again.
No one trusts a liar.

The end.